Mickey Mysteries

ABRACADABRA

Collect these Mickey Mysteries:

Mystery in Midair

Mystery of the Secret Treasure

and

Mystery of the Garbage Gang

Mickey Mysteries

ABRACADABRA

New York

Printed in the United States of America

First edition
1 3 5 7 9 10 8 6 4 2

Library of Congress Catalog Card Number: 2001090553
ISBN 0-7868-4452-3

For more Disney Press fun, visit www.disneybooks.com

Chapter 1

COMPANY'S COMING

It was eleven o'clock in the morning, and Mickey and Minnie were working busily at their desks. They had just solved a major case the day before, and both detectives were in a sunny mood. Minnie grinned as the telephone rang.

"Maybe that's Commissioner Mutton-chops, calling to thank us for our help on the case we just solved," Minnie suggested.

Mickey laughed. "Well, there's one way to find out," he replied.

Minnie scooped up the receiver eagerly.

"Mickey and Minnie Detective Agency," she said cheerfully.

"Good morning!" replied a deep voice. "This is Mr. Baker from Festival Pastries. I'm calling to make sure there's someone in the office this morning who can sign for the cakes."

"Cakes?" Minnie frowned. "What cakes?"

"The cakes you ordered!" Mr. Baker huffed. "Come now, miss—I don't have all day here. A week ago, you ordered two vanilla cakes, both to be decorated with the name of your agency in chocolate frosting. Whoever ordered them said they were for a party to celebrate your one-year anniversary." Mr. Baker sounded rather impatient.

"Hmm . . . this must be one of Mickey's ideas. . . . Could you hold on for just a moment?" Minnie turned to Mickey, who was huddled over his desk working, and smiled. "Oh, Mickey, what a great idea—a party to celebrate our first year in business together!"

"A party? To celebrate?" Mickey shook his head in confusion. "What are you talking about, Minnie?" he asked.

"Don't try to hide it," Minnie replied. "Mr. Baker is on the phone right now! He's sending someone over to deliver the cakes. . . . And I'll bet you've already ordered the flowers, too."

Mickey stared at his partner. "I didn't order any cakes, and I didn't organize any party. There must be some mistake. Let me talk to Mr. Baker."

Minnie handed the phone to Mickey. "Hello? Mr. Baker?" said Mickey.

"Yes, Baker here," the man replied.

"I'm sorry," Mickey told him, "but there must be some mistake. We haven't ordered any cakes."

"There's no mistake," Mr. Baker snapped. "Hold on a moment. . . . I'll read you the order. Here it is: two vanilla cakes for the Mickey and Minnie Detective Agency, to be delivered at 11:30 A.M., and aw, garsh, we were just about to bring them over—"

Suddenly Mickey realized he had heard the man's voice before. "Excuse me, sir, but have we met?" Mickey asked. When the voice on the other end of the line giggled, he knew he was right. "*Goofy!* Are you trying to play a joke on us?"

The giggle became a guffaw. "Ha, ha, ha! You both fell for it!" Goofy sounded delighted. "I can't believe you couldn't recognize my voice!"

"Well, not when you put a handkerchief over the phone receiver, Goofy!" Mickey replied with a chuckle.

Goofy gasped. "How did you know I put a handkerchief over the phone?" he asked, clearly disappointed.

"That's an old detective's trick, my friend!" Mickey said.

Minnie, who by now had figured out who the mysterious Mr. Baker really was, interrupted. "It may have been one of Goofy's sillier pranks, but it's really not a bad idea to have a party—"

Mickey nodded. "You're right, Minnie," he said. "Actually, how's this for an idea? To make up for tricking us, Goofy should bring us a big cake—with chocolate frosting!"

"Okay, okay," Goofy agreed, "as long as I get to have a slice, too. . . ."

"Of course," Mickey assured him. "It's always more fun to eat cake with friends!"

In less than half an hour, Goofy arrived at the office with a big white bakery box.

"Wow! This looks delicious!" Minnie said as they opened the box. Pink and white sugar roses sat on top of thick layers of creamy chocolate frosting.

"I can't wait to have a slice!" said Goofy, licking his lips.

Mickey smiled. He didn't know anyone who had a bigger sweet tooth than Goofy.

When they were done, Minnie stood up. "Well, now that it's lunchtime, I'm going home for a bit," she announced. "But I'm sure you won't want to eat lunch after that! Too bad, because I made you two some of my famous—"

"Wait a minute!" Mickey cut her off. "Don't think we're going to pass up lunch! We'll just eat it a little later than usual, that's all." Mickey grinned, then added, "You go on ahead, Minnie. Since Goofy is here, I'm going to have him help me put some documents in order in the top storage files. That is, if he can manage to get up out of his chair after all the cake he's eaten. We'll meet you at your place in half an hour or so."

"Great!" Minnie said, picking up her purse. "See you real soon!" she sang as she walked out the door.

"So," Goofy said once Minnie had left, "where are those files you needed help with?"

"To tell the truth," Mickey began, "I don't really need help with the files. I was hoping you would come with me somewhere."

"Where?" asked Goofy.

"Well," said Mickey mysteriously, "Minnie's birthday is a week from Saturday. I've been trying to think of a gift for her, something really special, but I couldn't come up with anything. Then I found out about a new amusement park called Enigma. It's a mystery theme park. I'm sure she'll love it! Will you come with me to the travel agency so I can get tickets?"

"Sure," said Goofy.

Mickey dug around in his desk and pulled out a pamphlet. "Take a look at this brochure—they have a wax museum, a haunted house, a ride on a ghost train, detective movies, and overnight accommodations in this gloomy castle. It sounds really spooky and fun! I'm going to get two tickets for the package deal. . . ."

Mickey got so excited about the mystery theme park that he lost track of time. Before he knew it, it was already 1:30.

"Oh, no!" he said, catching sight of the clock. "I didn't realize it was so late. Now there's no time to get the tickets before we meet Minnie for lunch. Oh, well. I guess we can just pass by the travel agency later in the afternoon."

"Okeydokey," Goofy replied. "Now let's go meet Minnie."

It was a short walk to the street where Minnie lived, and Mickey and Goofy arrived there in no time. But as they turned the corner, someone walked briskly past Goofy, shoving him. Goofy fell facedown on the pavement!

A large man with long, jet-black hair and a mustache, his face half covered by an enormous pair of black sunglasses, kept striding down the sidewalk. He didn't look back—and he didn't even say he was sorry!

"That was so rude!" Mickey fumed. He held out his hand and helped his friend to his feet.

"Tell me about it," Goofy agreed as he brushed himself off.

Goofy took a moment to straighten himself out, then the two friends headed up

Minnie's front walk. Mickey rang the door-bell. No answer. Mickey and Goofy looked at one another, worried. Without saying a word, they went around back to see if she was in the yard and hadn't heard the doorbell.

Suddenly, Detective Mickey broke into a run.

"Minnie!" he shouted. "Minnie! What's wrong?"

Minnie was lying on the ground. She was pale, and she seemed to be unconscious. Mickey felt her pulse and put his hand to her forehead.

"She doesn't have a fever. And her heart rate seems normal." Mickey turned to his friend. "Goofy, run and get a glass of water."

Goofy nodded and rushed into Minnie's house through the back door. When he returned, Mickey took the glass of water and immediately splashed it on Minnie's face.

Minnie's eyes popped open. "That's a nice way to thank someone who's invited you over for lunch!" she said, glaring at Mickey.

"But Minnie, you fainted and—"

"Fainted?" Minnie demanded. "I've never

fainted in my life. I can't believe you think you can fool me with your jokes twice in one day."

"Minnie, believe me," Goofy interrupted, "you were flat on your back in the grass—"

"That's enough!" Minnie cried, exasperated. "I know better than to believe you two jokers. Well, too bad for you—I officially take back my lunch invitation! And to think that I had even made chocolate pudding for you two. . . ."

"Oh, Minnie," Mickey protested, "you know how much I love chocolate pudding! Please let me have some—and besides, this is *not* one of our tricks!"

"Oh, okay," said Minnie, sighing. "Just give me a minute to clean myself up."

"Okay, you two, everybody to the table!" Detective Minnie called out through the door a few minutes later.

The three friends were munching happily on lunch when out of nowhere, Minnie exclaimed, "Have I ever told you two about Miss Agatha?"

"Who?" Mickey asked curiously.

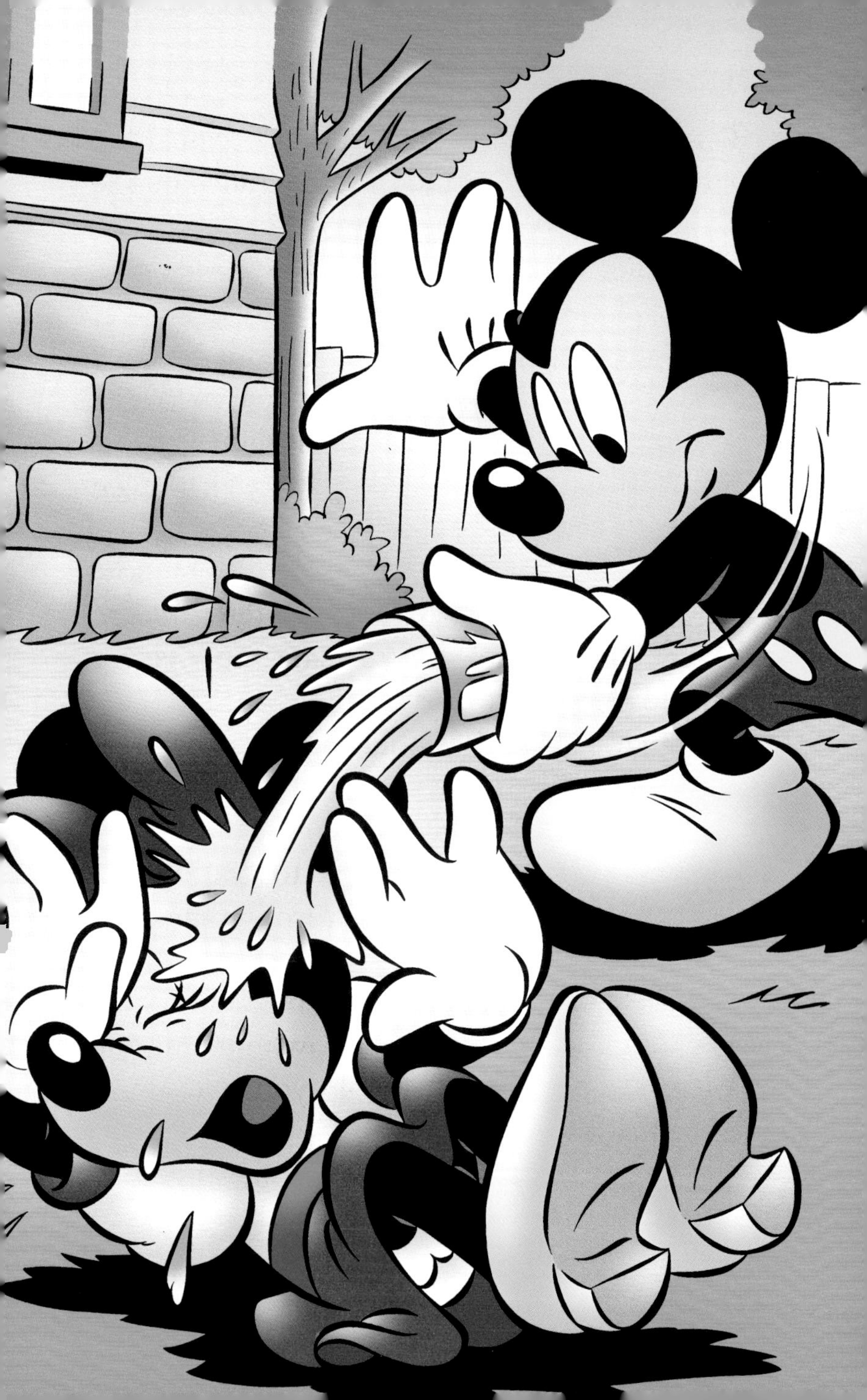

"Miss Agatha, my favorite teacher. She was almost like a second mother to me. She taught me so much—I owe her a lot. You could say that she helped create the Minnie that you know and love."

"Well, then, I guess we owe her a lot, too," Mickey said with a smile.

"Miss Agatha and I stayed in touch all these years," Minnie continued, "even though she lives far away."

"Now I remember," Mickey put in. "She invited you to go on vacation with her a few years ago, right?"

Minnie nodded. "That's right."

Mickey thought for a moment. "But I haven't heard you mention her in at least . . ."

"Two years exactly," Minnie finished for him. "It was two years ago that she got married and she and her husband started their trip around the world." Minnie gazed off into the distance dreamily. "If I can believe the postcards she's sent me, it's been an amazing trip. But I guess we'll hear all about it soon."

"What do you mean?" Mickey asked.

"Today I got a phone call. Mr. and Mrs.

Ruby, I mean Agatha and her husband Emilio, called to tell me that they will be arriving here today at seven-seventeen in the evening. They were hoping that I could come to the train station and pick them up because they have a lot of luggage. As far as I know, Emilio earned a lot of money during the course of his career and Agatha had no trouble adapting to a life of luxury. Anyway, it would be a shame if they had to take a taxi. . . ."

"How can we help?" Mickey asked.

"I was hoping you could give me a hand. I have an appointment at the dentist at seven o'clock. There's no way I can make it to the station in time."

Mickey snapped his fingers. "I get it! You want me and Goofy to go pick them up at the station."

Minnie smiled. "Exactly. You'll have no trouble recognizing them. They'll have four leather trunks and a few suitcases. They'll be waiting for you on the platform. Agatha will be wearing a white fur coat. . . ."

"Isn't it a bit hot for a fur coat?" Goofy asked.

"Heat is one thing, but fashion is another," Minnie replied. "Besides, it's not a real fur. Agatha's too much of an animal lover for that. More pudding?"

The three friends finished their lunch and then, with the excuse that he had an urgent errand to run, Mickey returned to the office. As planned, he passed by the travel agency. But as he was preparing to go inside, he realized that this surprise visit was going to ruin his plans. He couldn't buy the tickets unless he knew when he and Minnie were going on the trip, and he had no idea how long Agatha and Emilio were planning to stay. . . .

At 7:15, two minutes before the train was due to arrive, Mickey and Goofy met each other at the end of the station platform. When the train pulled into the station and travelers began filing off, Mickey and Goofy scanned the crowd closely looking for Minnie's friends. Several couples passed by, but none of them carried leather suitcases, and there was not a fake white fur coat in sight.

"Looks like they missed their train,"

Mickey commented once the platform was empty. "Oh well! Let's go tell Minnie that we couldn't find them."

As they walked away from the platform, the two friends heard an announcement on the loudspeaker:

"Mr. and Mrs. Ruby are waiting for Miss Minnie at track number two. I repeat: Mr. and Mrs. Ruby . . ."

Chapter 2

AT THE STATION

Mickey and Goofy headed straight for track two, where they saw a couple that fit the description Minnie had given them.

"Well, what could've happened to Minnie?" the woman in the white fur was asking the gentleman. "Why didn't she come to pick us up?"

"Excuse me, ma'am, you must be Agatha Ruby," Mickey said politely as he walked up to her. "Minnie asked us to come here and pick you up, but we were waiting at the wrong track. . . ."

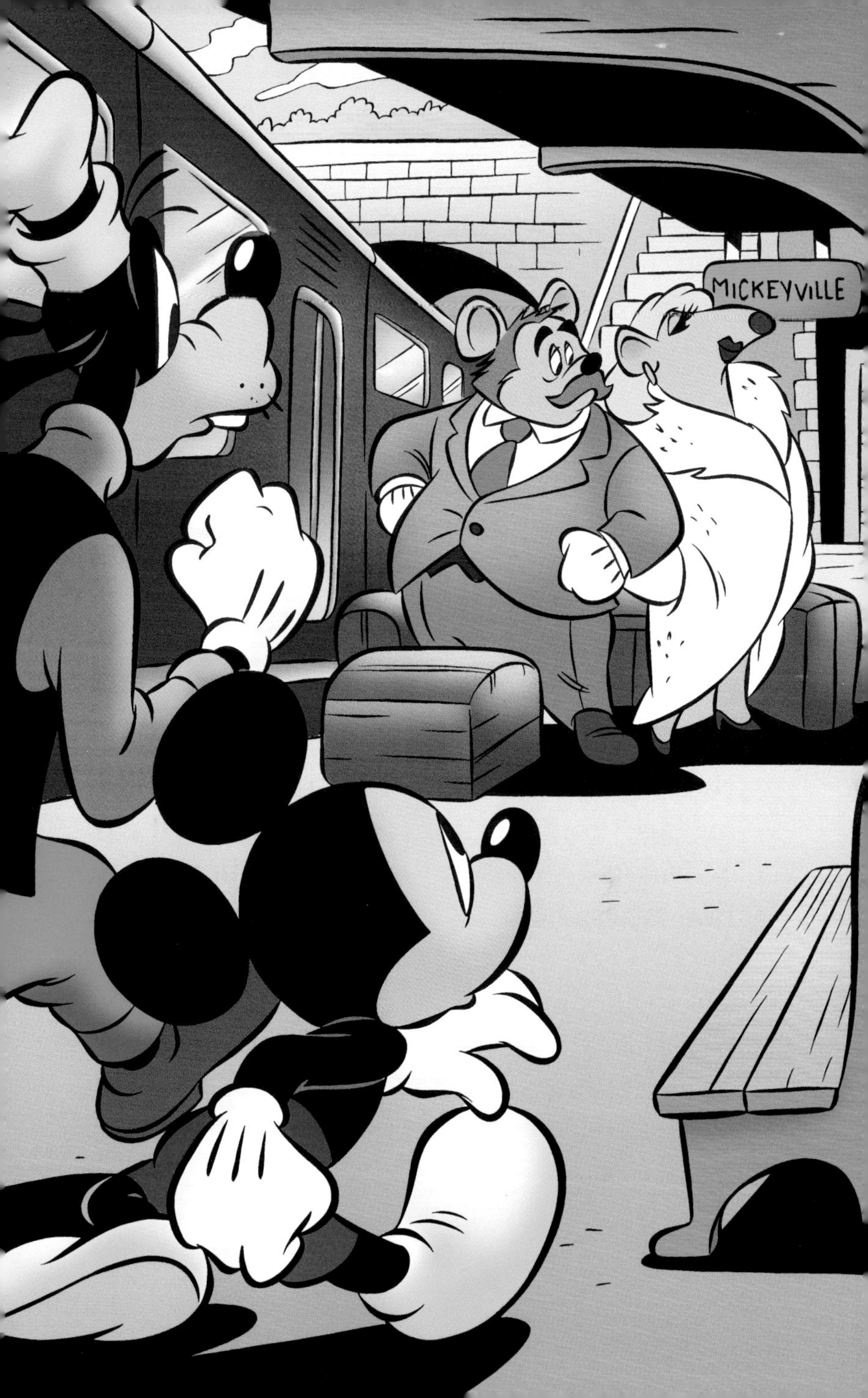
MICKEYVILLE

"Well, you should be more careful, young man," Mrs. Ruby replied with irritation. "We've been waiting a long time. Pick up our bags and let's get going!"

Although they were a little surprised by her tone of voice, Mickey and Goofy did as she asked. Mickey loaded the luggage into the trunk of the car, which became so full that it couldn't be closed. Finally, Mickey managed to wrestle it down with the help of two elastic cords. Minnie has no idea what's in store for her, Mickey thought as he struggled with the suitcases and leather trunks.

During the drive, Goofy remained silent. He'd had the tough job of carrying all of the luggage from the platform to Mickey's car, and now he was hot and tired. Plus, his toe hurt where he had dropped a trunk on it, and his vest was torn where it had been caught in the car door. He was getting cranky.

"Mickey, can you please drop me off at home?" Goofy asked as they drove through his neighborhood on the way to Minnie's house. "My favorite TV show starts at eight and I don't want to miss the beginning." Goofy shot Mickey a significant look.

"Fine," Mickey said and turned down the street where Goofy lived. But really, he was wishing that he could go home, too. Minnie's friends make me uncomfortable, he thought as he waved good-bye to Goofy and started for Minnie's house.

Minnie had already returned from her dentist appointment and was waiting for her guests on the front porch, concerned about the fact that they were late. When the car pulled up in front of her house, she rushed to open the car door and greet her friends.

"Hello, Agatha, so good to see you! Welcome, Emilio!" she exclaimed happily. "I hope you had a good trip!"

"I am very honored to meet you, Minnie!" Emilio gave a low bow. "Agatha has told me so much about you. I'm happy to finally make your acquaintance. It's a pity that your driver is so irresponsible. First he made us wait, and then—"

"My driver?" Minnie interrupted him.

"Mickey is not my driver! He's my business partner and one of my best friends!"

"Oh, *excuse* me." Emilio's jaw dropped open. "I was confused! Pardon me, young man. But, if you're not a driver, what sort of work do you do?"

"You never told me about your job, Minnie," Agatha said primly.

"A year ago, Mickey and I opened a private detective agency," Minnie explained. "We solve a lot of cases."

"Really?" Emilio exclaimed. "Well, I had no idea. Extraordinary . . . I'm very happy for you both. And now, if you don't mind, could you show us to our room? I have to admit that I feel very drained after our long journey."

"Of course!" Minnie said warmly. "What was I thinking? Follow me, I've prepared a room for you on the second floor, the prettiest room in the house. The window looks out over the Rosamonds' beautiful garden. I hope you'll have the chance to meet them— they're very nice."

"We should certainly organize a party and invite the city's most important people,"

Agatha replied with a smile.

"Speaking of parties," Mickey interrupted, "Goofy invited us to a party at his house tomorrow evening. Please come with us," he added, turning to the Rubys.

"With pleasure. My trunks are full of evening gowns, and I'd love to have the chance to wear one of them!" Agatha's eyes twinkled with enthusiasm.

"Agatha!" Emilio reproached her, then laughed. "My wife does love her gowns . . . as you can tell by the huge amount of luggage we've brought with us!"

Minnie grinned. "And speaking of your luggage," she said, "Mickey and I should start taking yours up to your room!"

Minnie nudged her friend toward the mountain of baggage. Mickey lifted one of the trunks to his shoulders, staggering from the weight.

This thing isn't filled with clothes . . . it's filled with rocks! he thought. Poor Minnie, I don't think she'll have a very good time with these houseguests of hers. They seem pretty snobby to me.

Mickey started the long climb up the stairs to the "prettiest room in the house," as Minnie called it.

When he had finished carrying up all the bags, detective Mickey met Minnie in the kitchen. She was preparing dinner for her guests, who had gone to their room to rest for a bit.

He snuck a piece of carrot out of the salad.

"How are you going to handle them all by yourself?" Mickey asked, munching the carrot. "Don't forget that we have work to do on our investigations!"

"I know," Minnie replied. "We'll have to wait and see how things work out. . . ."

"Whatever you say, Minnie." Mickey sighed as he watched his dream of taking Minnie to the mystery park evaporate into thin air. Who knew when Minnie's world-traveling guests would decide it was time to move on?

Chapter 3

MAGIC IN THE DARK

The next evening, Minnie and the Rubys were the first to arrive at Goofy's party.

Emilio was carrying one of their massive suitcases, which was stuffed full of who knows what. His wife was dressed very elegantly. She was wearing a black evening gown and lots of sumptuous jewelry: a very valuable diamond necklace and a collection of gold bracelets that clinked together cheerfully every time she moved her arm.

"Oh, Agatha," Minnie exclaimed, "you'll be the belle of the ball! But I was wondering—

don't you worry about thieves when you wear all that expensive jewelry?"

"Oh, but here we're among friends. I'm not worried at all," Agatha said with a toss of her head. "Emilio, my darling, perhaps now is the time to tell everyone what we have brought with us. I don't think anyone here knows yet about your special talent."

Emilio smiled and immediately opened the heavy suitcase. He then extracted a series of objects and placed them carefully on the coffee table.

"You must understand," he explained with a modest air, "that for a few years I've had a little hobby. I like to do magic tricks. Every time we find ourselves at a party, I love to practice my tricks in front of people. But I never reveal my secrets! Sir," he said, turning to Goofy, "do you think your guests would enjoy seeing some of my tricks?"

"I'm sure they would," Goofy replied, thrilled about the unexpected entertainment for his guests. "Just give me a minute to make sure everyone is here before you start the show."

One by one, the guests began to arrive. Minnie introduced all the visitors to Mr. and Mrs. Ruby and soon everyone was mingling and chatting. So far, the evening was going smoothly, and Goofy was feeling very satisfied.

Finally, when all the guests had arrived, Emilio put on a black cape. Goofy helped him clear off a table, and Emilio set himself up behind it.

"Ladies and gentlemen," he announced, "I will begin with a few card tricks."

Emilio Ruby asked three guests to pick cards out of a deck. Once they had looked at the cards, Emilio put the cards back in the deck and shuffled. With surprising ability, Emilio Ruby picked cards out of the deck, finding the exact same cards the guests had chosen before! Everyone was amazed.

Then Agatha handed her husband a top hat. Emilio quickly passed his hand back and forth over the hat, and twenty green scarves appeared out of nowhere. He shoved the scarves back into the hat and pulled them out again, and the audience gasped when they saw that the green scarves had turned to yellow!

The audience exploded into applause. For an amateur, Emilio was terrific!

"And now," the magician declared in a solemn tone, "I would like to present you with my most incredible trick, the highlight of my show! Agatha, if you please."

From the trunk, Agatha extracted several wooden panels and placed them one after

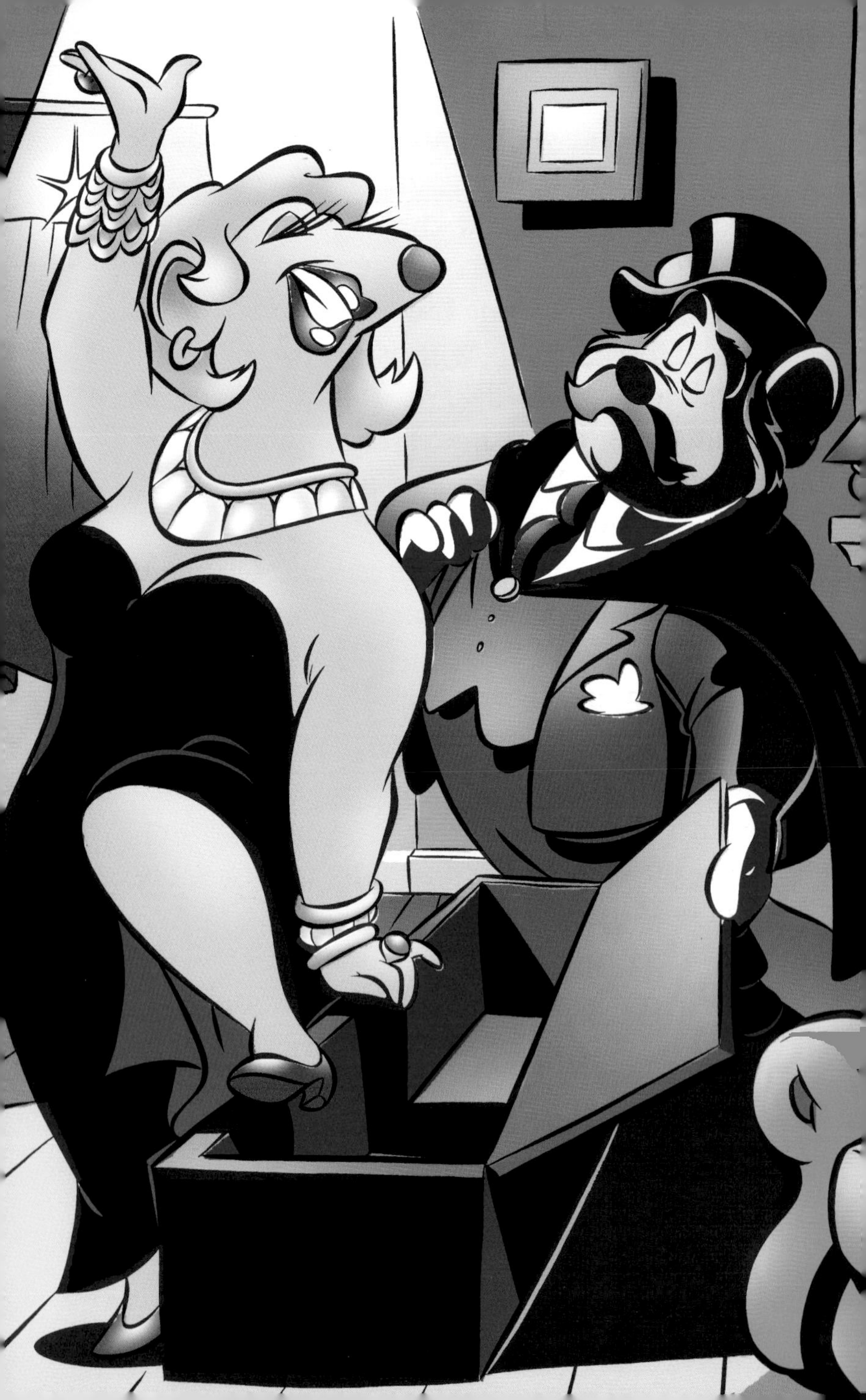

the other in front of her husband. In a flash, Emilio assembled the panels into a large black box. He opened the lid and signaled to his wife. Agatha came forward, lifted the hem of her long black dress and, with an elegant gesture, stepped into the magic box. She stretched out on her back inside the box. She waved, and her gold bracelets jingled together merrily. Without a word, Emilio closed the lid of the box.

The audience sat there, perfectly still and silent, waiting to see what would happen next.

Emilio murmured a few magic words. Then he unraveled the scarves that he had drawn out of the top hat and covered the magic box. A moment later, the lights in the room went out and the guests found themselves immersed in total darkness. Someone let out a shriek. Was this part of the trick?

Chapter 4

SOMETHING'S NOT RIGHT

Mickey stood up quickly and tried to reassure the guests. "Don't worry, everyone!" he cried. "There must be just a little unexpected problem with the power supply. I'll try to turn the electricity back on so Emilio can continue his show."

Mickey headed for the kitchen to find the fuse box. In the meantime, the guests sat stock-still, worried for poor Agatha shut up in total darkness inside the magic box.

Then, just as suddenly as they had gone off, the lights came on again. Everyone looked at one another, blinking their eyes against the bright light. In a great hurry, Emilio opened the lid of the magic case. His wife burst out immediately, red as a tomato, overheated and disheveled.

"What happened?" she asked, visibly upset. "Why did you just leave me closed up in there?"

"I'm so sorry, Agatha. The lights went out just as I locked you in, and I couldn't manage to unlock it in the dark. But—but where are your jewels?" he asked suddenly, his voice trembling.

Agatha shrieked. She leaned over the box and began to search frantically for her missing jewelry. Then she stood up.

"They're gone!" she exclaimed, trembling like a leaf.

"Calm down, dear," her husband said. "How could they have just disappeared? You were closed inside and no one could open the box except me!"

"I don't know what to believe," Agatha replied, on the verge of tears. "All I know is that my jewels have disappeared."

"Why don't we call the police?" Goofy suggested.

"The police?" Emilio repeated. "Yes, good idea. Even though I am afraid that they'll think we're crazy. Think about it: a woman closed in a magic box is robbed of all her valuable jewels," he said.

"Was your jewelry insured?" Goofy asked, turning to Agatha. He felt terrible that someone had been robbed at his party.

"Yes, of course," Emilio replied. "They're antiques. Agatha inherited them from her grandmother. They mean a great deal to her."

Distressed, Mrs. Ruby sat down on the edge of the couch. She stared ahead blankly, without saying a word.

"In the meantime," Goofy asked, "where's Mickey? Why didn't he come back after turning the lights back on?"

Goofy trotted into the kitchen, but returned immediately to the doorway in the living room.

"What's happened?" one of the guests asked. Goofy had gone white as a sheet.

"Mickey just found Minnie passed out on the kitchen floor!" he cried.

They revived poor Minnie by pinching her cheeks. As soon as she woke up, she began to laugh and look around her in surprise.

"What am I doing on the floor in front of the refrigerator?" she asked.

"You just fainted," Mickey told her.

"Really? I don't remember a thing," Minnie

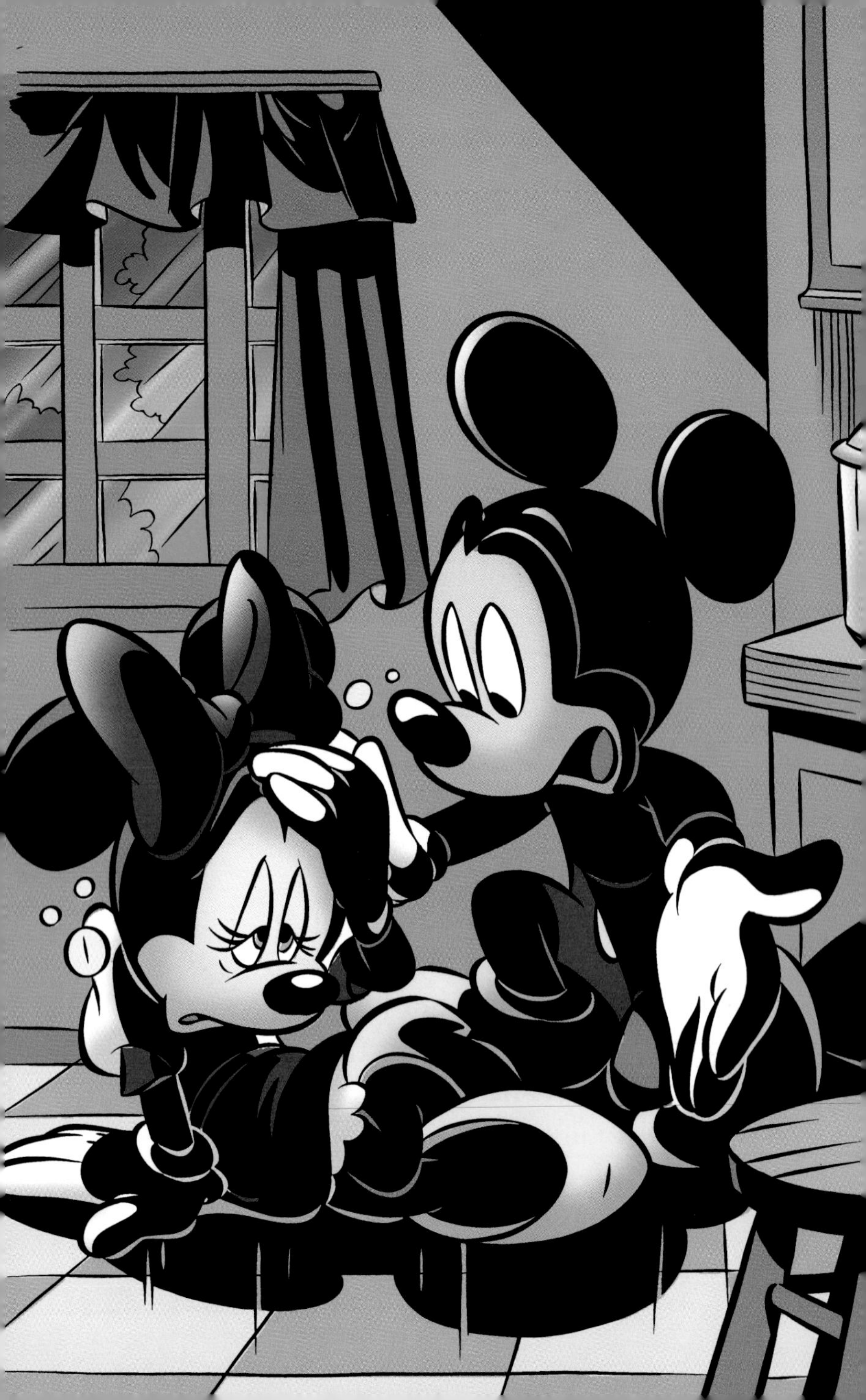

replied as she struggled to her feet.

"Maybe you need to eat something," Mickey suggested, frowning. This is the second time in two days that Minnie has fallen in a dead faint and woken up with no memory of what had happened to her, he thought.

Mickey held Minnie up by her arm because her legs were still too weak to stand on their own. Together, they hobbled into the living room. Meanwhile, the guests had formed a circle around Agatha, while her husband continued to try to comfort her.

"Don't worry, my darling," Emilio said soothingly. "I'll buy you another necklace just like it, I promise! The important thing is that you're safe. You know that you are my most precious jewel. Nothing matters more to me than your life and your safety."

In between sobs, Agatha nodded. Then she grabbed the handkerchief from her husband's hands and dried her eyes.

"Fine," she exclaimed, "now let's get out and find those thieves! These criminals will not go unpunished."

"Yes, dear," Emilio replied gently. "But let's

leave it to the professionals. Isn't that right, Mickey? After all, it's your job to track down thieves, isn't it?"

"Oh, right—of course," Mickey agreed. He wondered if the Rubys' visit would last forever, now that the jewels were gone. "But really, there's nothing unusual about blowing a fuse. Maybe the jewels just slid under some piece of furniture when it was dark. For the moment, there's no real reason to worry."

"Would anyone like a nice, hot drink?" Goofy asked, trying to make his guests feel comfortable. But the room stayed silent— nobody was in the mood for a party anymore. A few minutes later, the guests were putting on their coats. They thanked their host and left in a hurry.

Goofy shook his head as he watched everyone leave. What a disaster, he thought.

Chapter 5

UNDER STRICT
SURVEILLANCE

Early the next day, Mickey called
Commissioner Muttonchops's office to tell
him what had happened the night before.
The commissioner listened closely to everything the detective had to say, then asked,
"Did you check to see whether the jewels
were underneath the bottom lining of the
magic box?"

"Yes, of course," Mickey assured him. "I
went over the whole house with a fine-tooth
comb, but I didn't find anything."

The commissioner paused a moment, then said, "You know, it seems clear to me that the thief was one of the guests at the party."

"Yes, I think so, too," Mickey agreed. "But all of the guests are friends I've known for a long time. I find it hard to suspect any of them."

"Let's wait a few days," Commissioner

Muttonchops suggested. "Let's see if this thief makes a false move."

"Good idea," the detective replied. "I'll keep you posted if there are any new developments, Commissioner. Whatever happens, we can't leave this case open."

"Good-bye, Mickey," the commissioner said. "Good luck!"

As he walked to the office, Mickey was deep in thought. But he wasn't thinking about the case—he was worrying about his partner. Minnie really hadn't been herself for the past few days. And no wonder. Every day after she worked at the agency, she rushed home to make dinner for Agatha and Emilio. She had dark circles under her eyes and seemed tired all the time. Mickey was worried for his friend, and he didn't know how to tell her to take better care of herself.

But when he arrived at the detective agency, Minnie seemed to be in high spirits.

"Good morning, Mickey," she exclaimed. "Guess what! The Rosamonds invited us to a party at their house on Sunday. They invited the Rubys as well. Isn't that great news? Now

ave a night off from taking care of
he added with a small sigh.

nie," her partner said gently, "I've been
wanting to speak to you about this for a few
days, but I didn't know what to say. You've
been waiting on Agatha and Emilio hand and
foot, and I'm worried that you'll wear yourself out."

"Maybe you're right, Mickey," Minnie
admitted. "Then again, it's not like they'll be
staying with me forever. . . ."

Mickey looked at her a moment, then
shrugged. "Whatever you think," he said.
"Either way, I'd love to go with you to the
Rosamonds' party on Sunday. Do you think
that Emilio will try his disappearing lady trick
again?"

Minnie laughed. "I doubt it. Not after the
lady didn't disappear—but her jewels did!"

Sunday evening, Mickey and Goofy picked
up Minnie and the Rubys.

Once again, Agatha looked absolutely
splendid. Her husband had bought her some
new jewelry to console her and she was

wearing a magnificent green dress. Her hair was swept up in an elegant bun decorated with ribbons that matched her dress.

"This evening," she whispered to Mickey, "Emilio won't be doing his magic act. He didn't think it was a good idea after what happened the other night at Goofy's house."

"Good idea," Mickey said. Then he politely added, "May I say that you look very elegant this evening."

For the first time since they'd met, Agatha smiled at Mickey.

The Rosamonds' house was flooded with light. As the guests arrived, a butler accompanied them to the top of the majestic staircase and announced their name as they made their entrance into the mansion.

The first room was dedicated to the buffet. The tables were covered with exquisite delicacies like asparagus tarts, vegetable pastries, and stuffed mushroom caps. In the second room, a jazz band played as guests whirled around the room.

The men were in tuxedoes and each

woman looked more elegant than the next. Mrs. Rosamond was wearing a splendid light blue silk gown and a fabulous diamond choker. On her head was a beautiful tiara. Rings and bracelets adorned her hands.

"My dear friends," said a warm voice moving across the room toward Mickey and Minnie, "it's so wonderful to see you! And these, my dear Minnie, these must be your guests, Mr. and Mrs. Ruby. Good evening, it's a pleasure to make your acquaintance. In fact, Mr. Ruby, I have already heard that you are an extraordinarily gifted magician—"

"Oh, Mrs. Rosamond," Emilio responded as he bowed gallantly before the hostess, "I am honored that you have heard of my love for the magical arts. But your guests here tonight, well, they are much too prestigious and well-traveled to enjoy the tricks of such an amateur as myself."

Mrs. Rosamond smiled. "As you wish, my dear. But you will all have to excuse me for a moment," she continued, "some new guests have arrived. I must make them feel welcome. Please, help yourselves to the hors d'oeuvres."

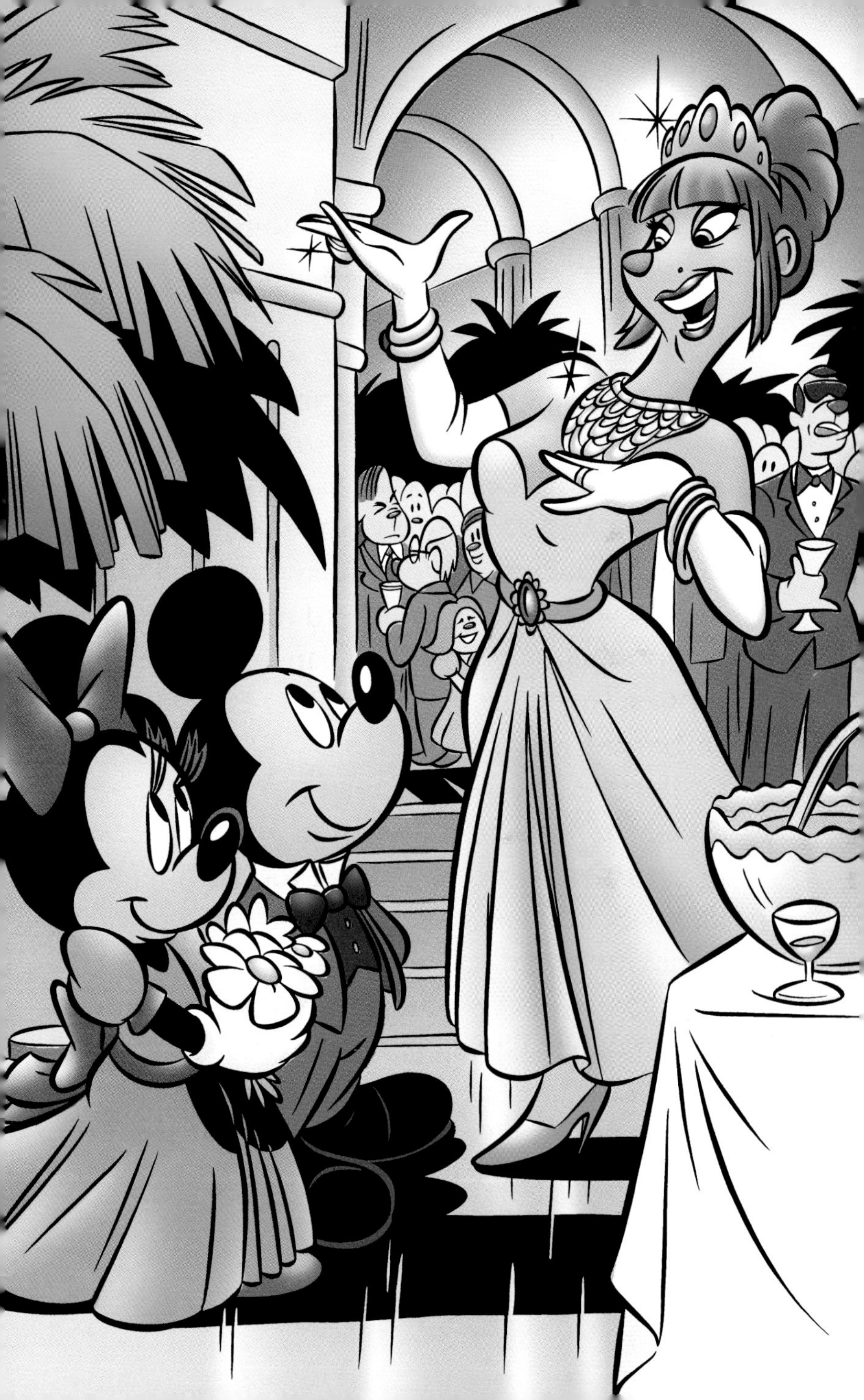

Meanwhile, a few steps away, Mickey kept a discreet eye on the Rubys as they crossed the room to sample the buffet. He kept a particularly sharp eye on Agatha, whose jewels would certainly attract any thief. If any suspicious characters tried to approach her, Mickey would be able to identify them immediately. Still, questions were swimming around in the detective's head. For example, why did Agatha continue to wear such valuable jewels even after she'd been robbed the other night? Why hadn't they returned to Goofy's house to look for Agatha's necklace, especially since it had such great sentimental value? No, Mickey did not want to lose sight of these two strange characters. He had even asked Goofy to keep an eye on them as well, in case someone came to chat with him and he got distracted.

But just as these thoughts were passing through Mickey's mind, the room was suddenly plunged into total darkness!

Chapter 6

WHERE IS MINNIE?

A few screams rang out, then the guests began to whisper among themselves. Mickey raised his voice and quieted everyone.

"Don't worry, there must be a failure at the central electrical plant. The garden has gone dark, too. I'll go and find out what's happened. Please, don't move, stay where you are. We don't want anyone to get hurt." Mickey rushed off to find a telephone.

Unfortunately, the guests did not seem to find Mickey's speech reassuring. Those friends who had also been at Goofy's house the week before were particularly disturbed. But soon silence fell over the room as the guests waited anxiously for the lights to be restored.

Seconds became minutes. Nothing. The guests, standing in the dark, were becoming increasingly terrified when, all of a sudden, a shriek echoed throughout the large room.

"Stop! Help! My jewels—the lights, please!"

The voice, recognizable to all, belonged to the mistress of the house, Mrs. Rosamond.

A moment later, the chandeliers came back on. Squinting against the sudden brightness, the guests remained frozen in place for a few moments. Then everyone turned to look at their hostess, who was standing at the center of the room, pale as a ghost. The diamond choker and the other jewels that Mrs. Rosamond had been wearing were gone. The guests gathered around her, but no one dared to speak.

In that moment Mickey reentered the great room. He seemed very annoyed.

"Well," he grumbled, "the power plant in

this neighborhood certainly isn't very dependable!"

Mrs. Rosamond slowly began to regain her courage. She turned to the detective and said, "My jewelry is missing! There is a thief among us!"

Mickey looked around the room. Everyone at the party was a friend of his . . . and of Mrs. Rosamond. "Please, try to remain calm. These are our friends," Mickey reminded her.

"Where is Emilio?" Agatha asked suddenly. "I have to tell him what has happened. Twice in two weekends! This city certainly doesn't seem very safe."

"Don't worry, Agatha. Mickey and I will find your husband right now," Goofy assured her. Goofy turned to Mickey. "Come on," he said, and started up the stairs. He showed Mickey a door on the second floor.

"I saw Mr. Ruby go into that room about half an hour ago," he explained to his friend.

Detective Mickey approached the door silently and entered a beautiful bedroom. The room was completely dark, but the light coming in from the hall was enough to allow

Mickey to distinguish the outline of a figure on one of the two twin beds. Mickey touched the light switch. In the yellow light of the lamp, he saw a man lying down . . . perfectly still.

"Emilio!" he whispered.

No response.

The detective approached the bed.

"Emilio!" he tried again, louder this time.

Emilio opened his eyes slowly, then closed them tightly, stunned by the bright light.

"What's happening?" he asked in a groggy voice. It sounded as though he had just woken from a deep sleep.

"Emilio," Mickey repeated, "something terrible has happened. Mrs. Rosamond's jewels have disappeared!"

Emilio scrambled to his feet.

"Oh, no! Again!" he exclaimed. "This city is full of thieves!"

"I think your wife wants to see you," Mickey said. "She seems upset."

"Yes, of course. I'm on my way." When he was halfway out the door, Emilio stopped and turned back. "You know," he explained, clearly embarrassed, "I fall asleep at parties fairly often. My wife loves to go out, but I have different tastes. For me there's nothing better than a relaxing night at home, snoozing on the couch. But, to make her happy, every once in a while I indulge her, only she's more energetic than me. At ten o'clock, sleepiness overcomes me and I can't keep my eyes open anymore. . . . Especially if she won't let me do my magic tricks," he added.

Mickey and Goofy nodded. Then Mickey led the way down the hall.

"Here he is!" the detective exclaimed triumphantly when he reentered the room where the guests were waiting. "We've found Mr. Ruby! He was fast asleep upstairs." Mickey looked around the room, adding, "Minnie, why don't you get him something refreshing to drink. Something to help perk him up. Minnie?" he repeated. His friend and partner was nowhere to be found.

"Oh no! I hope she hasn't disappeared again!" Goofy exclaimed nervously. Then, leaning close to Mickey, he whispered, "I kept a close eye on Emilio and Agatha, just like you asked me. Agatha stayed on the couch and Emilio left the room after asking the waiter to bring him a chamomile tea. But now that I think about it, I wasn't keeping an eye on Minnie as I should have been. . . ." He shook his head.

Mickey placed his hand gently on Goofy's arm.

"Don't worry," he consoled him. "Minnie

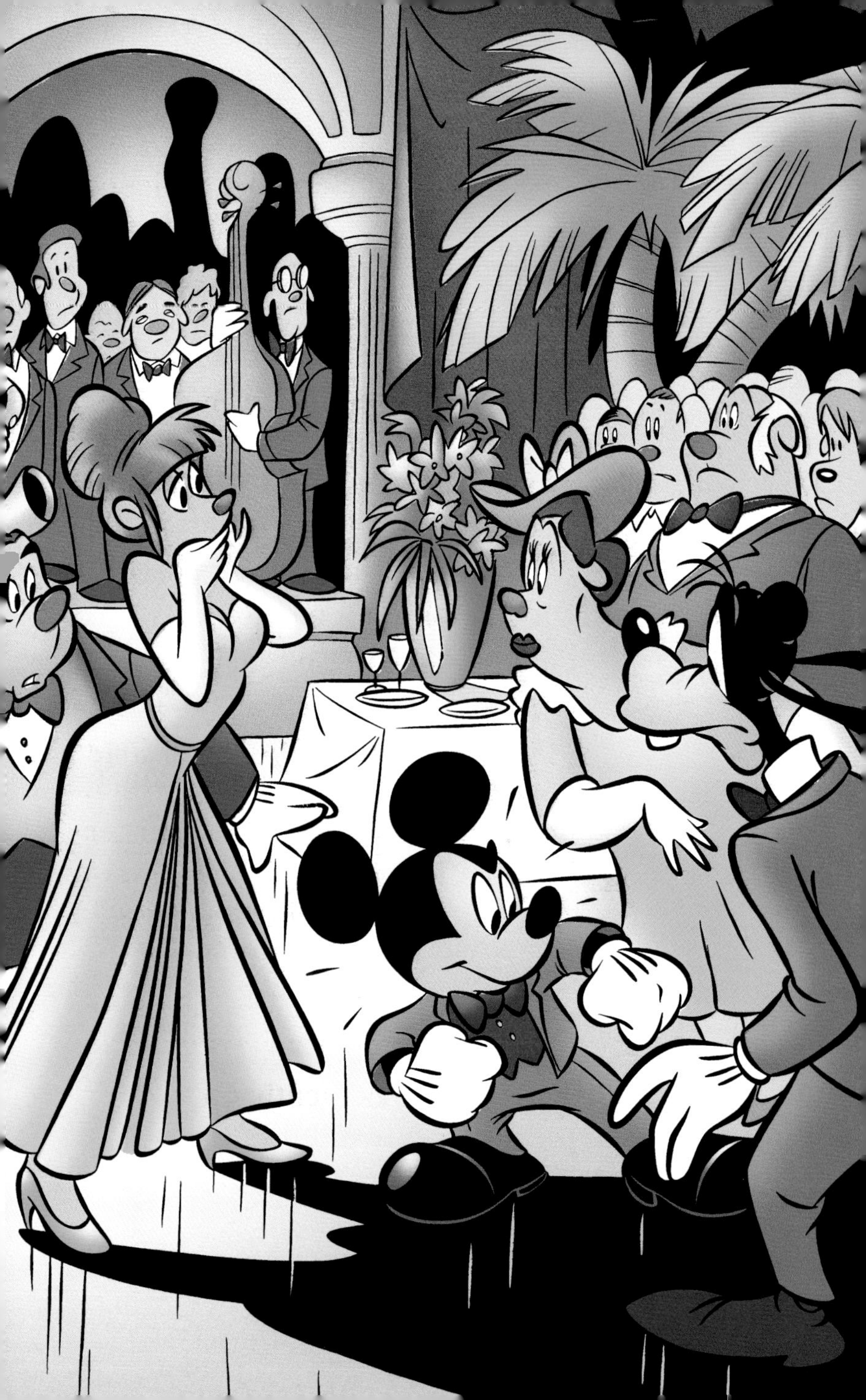

probably went to look for a waiter to get something to drink."

The two friends walked toward the kitchen. But several of the guests who had overheard their conversation followed them, curious as to Minnie's whereabouts. In a moment the corridor was full of people, so much so that it was impossible to move backward or forward. Once again, Mickey had to take the situation into his own hands.

"My dear friends," he said calmly, "please, go back to the main hall. Goofy and I will go look for Minnie on our own. Please . . ."

As the guests filed back into the main hall, Mickey and Goofy entered the kitchen. They pushed through the swinging door, which closed behind them with a long, sinister creak.

On the floor they saw a familiar figure.

"Minnie!" Mickey cried.

Chapter 7

AN UNUSUAL SUSPECT

Detective Mickey ran to his friend's side, leaned down, and began gently slapping her cheeks. He took her up in his arms . . . and slowly Minnie's eyes began to open.

"Mickey!" she said. "Put me down right this instant! You've been acting so weird lately. The other day you threw a glass of water in my face. Now tonight you are carrying me around like a baby. Are you sure you're all right?" she asked, a note of irritation in her voice. "Maybe you should see a doctor—"

"Really, Minnie," Mickey interrupted gently,

"you're the one who's been acting weird. We keep finding you passed out in the strangest places. You disappear in the most crucial moments, and then when you wake up all you do is complain! Could you be suffering from some sort of nervous exhaustion?"

Mickey helped his friend to a nearby chair.

"I don't understand," Minnie replied. "I didn't faint, not today, not yesterday, not last week. I was in the kitchen because I wanted to ask the waiter—wait a minute, what did I want to ask him?" She shook her head, suddenly disturbed. "I'm drawing a blank. I remember walking out of thc main room, I remember walking down the hall toward the kitchen, and then . . ."

"And then you fainted," Mickey finished for her. "Tomorrow I'm taking you to the doctor for a checkup."

"Do you really think that's necessary?" Minnie bit her lip.

"Minnie," Mickey intervened, "while you were unconscious, something terrible happened. The jewels that Mrs. Rosamond was wearing were stolen!"

"No—" Minnie protested, looking from Mickey to Goofy, then back again. When she saw the serious looks on their faces, she gulped. "Really?"

"Yes, really. And there are some coincidences that are puzzling me," Mickey said reflectively. "First, all this mess started when the Rubys got to town. But what's happened here tonight has shown that they are above suspicion. Emilio couldn't be simultaneously upstairs in a bedroom and down here shutting off the electricity."

"And Agatha must be innocent. When the lights went out she was sitting right near me, and I didn't see her move once," Goofy added. "But now we have to try and figure out why Minnie is acting so strangely," he concluded, turning to his friend with a worried look on his face.

"Right!" Mickey exclaimed. "Minnie hasn't been herself at all. Usually, her feet are on the ground—but lately her head has been in the clouds!"

"Wait a minute," Minnie interrupted. She pushed back her chair and stood up. "I can't have my feet on the ground and my head in the clouds at the same time! It's not like I'm as tall as Goofy!"

Minnie began to laugh heartily at her own joke.

Her two friends stared at each other, stupefied. Now Minnie was *really* acting bizarre!

Looking around the kitchen, Mickey noticed a glass that had been placed on the dish rack by the sink to dry. He filled the glass with water and then, with a decisive gesture, tossed it in Minnie's face.

Minnie immediately went silent. Her eyes widened, her jaw dropped—she was as still as a statue. Mickey came closer to her and placed his hand softly on her shoulder. No response.

"Minnie!" he called her name gently. "Minnie, it's me, Mickey. Are you all right?" he asked.

Still no response.

Then, all of a sudden, everything returned to normal. Minnie turned toward her partner and, in her usual voice, responded, "I'm just fine, and you? I don't know about you two, but I'm starving!"

And then, as if nothing had happened, she turned on her heel and strode out of the kitchen.

Out in the main hall, guests were milling about in total confusion.

While Mickey, Minnie, and Goofy had been in the kitchen talking, someone had called

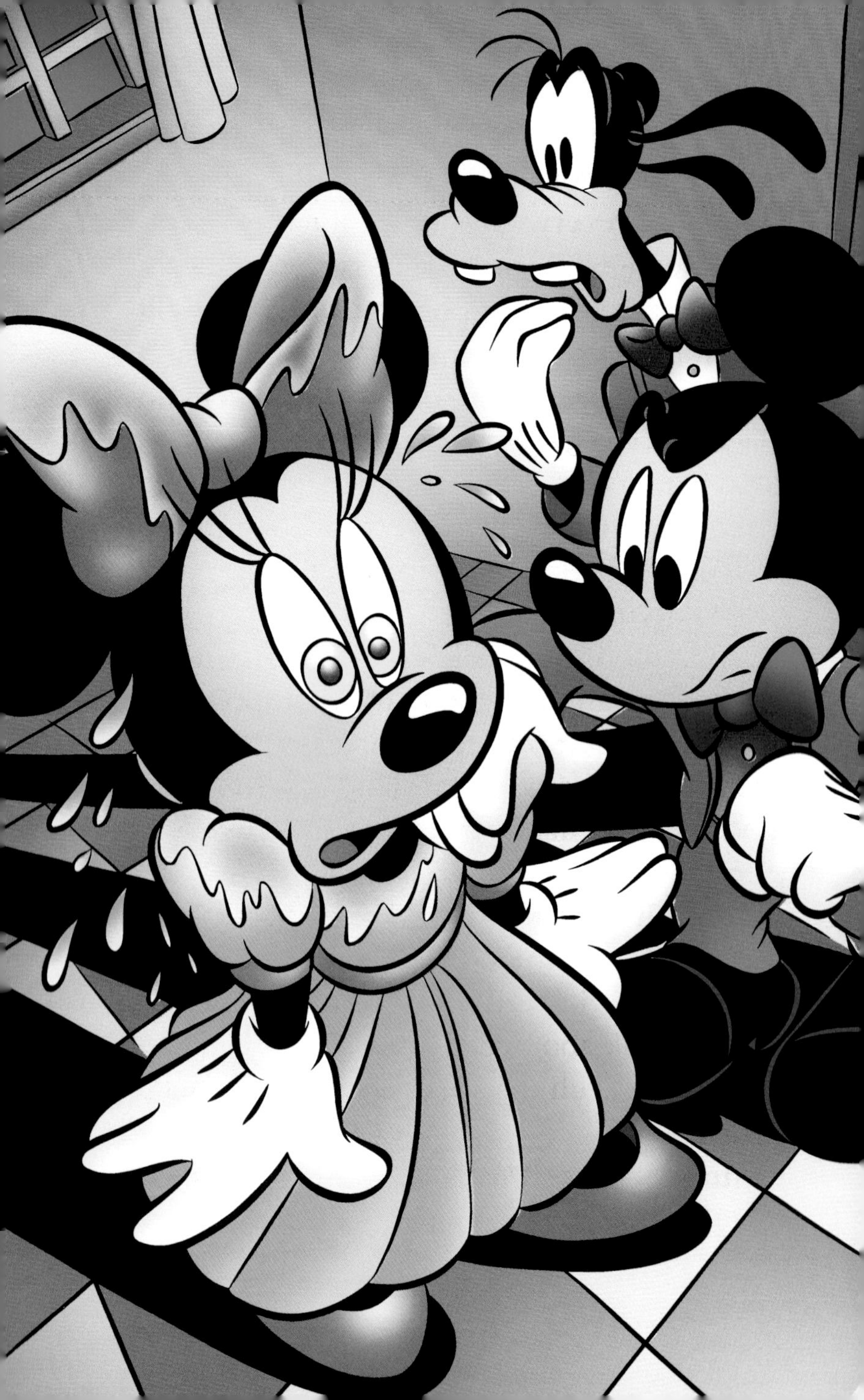

the police. Commissioner Muttonchops had arrived in person.

"I think everyone should go home and get a good night's rest," Commissioner Muttonchops suggested. "Let the police handle this situation."

The guests didn't need to be told twice. They quickly gathered their coats and said good-bye to Mrs. Rosamond.

"Well," she said as she closed the front door, "this was the worst party I've ever thrown in my life."

The next morning, when the phone rang at the Mickey and Minnie Detective Agency, it was Mickey who picked it up. "Oh, good morning, Commissioner!" he said. "How are you?"

"I'm all right," Muttonchops replied. "This wave of thefts that seems to be spreading over the city is bothering me, though. What do you think about all of this?"

"Well . . . uh . . ." Mickey hedged, "let's see . . ."

Muttonchops frowned at the receiver.

Mickey was known to be someone who spoke his mind, whatever the consequences.

"You're not alone, I take it?" Muttonchops asked.

"Er—exactly," the detective said hurriedly, relieved. "Maybe I should stop by later and see you?"

"Certainly," the commissioner replied. "I'll see you later today."

An hour later, Mickey was seated across from Muttonchops. Once again, they went over the facts of the case.

"You see, ever since we found Minnie passed out in her garden, strange things have been happening," Mickey explained. "She's always tired and she really doesn't seem to be herself. . . ."

"Are you saying that you think there's a connection between these thefts and Minnie's strange behavior?" the commissioner asked.

Mickey hesitated, then nodded. "I'm afraid so," he admitted. "Although it seems so unlike her. . . . Oh, I don't know what to believe anymore—the whole situation is bizarre! Who would've thought that a detective like Minnie could ever be suspected of robbery?"

"Come on, Mickey, don't give up hope yet," Muttonchops urged. "I'm sure there's a reasonable explanation for all of this."

"You're right," Mickey admitted. "Still, I'd like to try an experiment. I suggested to Minnie that she organize a party at my house for Friday evening to try and cheer everyone up and help them forget the last two disastrous parties. I would like to invite you to be my guest. Maybe together we can solve the mystery."

"Great idea," Muttonchops said warmly. "I'll post Inspector Swift in the yard to watch the comings and goings. Mickey, you should be Minnie's shadow. I'll keep a close eye on the guests in the living room."

"Sounds good," the detective said approvingly. "In any case, we can't let on that we're conducting an investigation. We don't want people to worry. And we don't want Minnie to find out!"

"Certainly," Muttonchops's face was serious. "You can count on me and on Inspector Swift."

As he left the commissioner's office, Mickey passed by the travel agency and felt a sense of deep disappointment. When would he be able to surprise Minnie with the special trip he had planned? It was only a few days until her birthday—and everything had turned upside down!

Chapter 8

THE FIRST CLUES

It was late in the evening and Mickey was in the office surrounded by a mountain of documents. Thanks to the recent rash of jewelry thefts in the last few days, Mickey hadn't had time to keep up with filing the faxes and arrest warrants sent to the agency. Mickey sighed and turned on the computer. He would do the filing later, right now he wanted to connect to the Internet. He logged on at the international detectives' site and saw several ugly mug shots materialize on the screen. Most of those faces were already familiar to him.

"Not much here that I haven't seen before," he grumbled.

He decided to print out the shots of the few faces he didn't recognize. Then he read the suspects' names out loud: "B. Lou Diamond, O. Pal, S. F. Ire . . ."

He was interrupted by the sound of the fax machine.

"It's a new message. . . ." Mickey said, peering at the paper as it scrolled out of the machine. "Let's see, here. . . . Look, another warrant for the arrest of—P. Earl. . . . Who's that?" Mickey scanned to the bottom. "He's a jewel thief. . . ." The detective looked at the other mug shots he had downloaded. "What a pile! Let's see what crimes these other guys are accused of, maybe I can organize them. This one supposedly robbed a jewelry store, this one is a jewel thief, this one stole precious stones, this one is . . . another jewel thief! Seems like an epidemic! I wonder if these scoundrels don't have something to do with our little problem?"

Since there was no room on his crowded desk, Mickey tacked the mug shots to the wall above his workspace. The faces of the individuals sought in connection with the jewelry thefts were incredibly similar. In fact, they appeared to be photographs of the same person in different disguises—sometimes with a different wig or a fake mustache, sometimes with a different hair color.

"I can't believe it!" Mickey exclaimed. "This has got to be our man. But why does he have all these different names? Let's see here: B. Lou Diamond, O. Pal . . ."

The detective thought for a moment. The names and surnames that the thief had used had something in common! They all contained the name of a precious stone! B. Lou Diamond was blue diamond, O. Pal, opal, and the others were sapphire and pearl. "This thief is seriously into jewels. Well," Mickey growled to the photographs on the wall, "you're not going to get away with it this time. There's no way I'll stand by and let Minnie take the heat for your crimes!"

Mickey began getting ready for the party on Friday morning. He set up a comfortable lawn

chair behind a hedge near the front door. He knew Inspector Swift would be glad to have a seat. After all, the party might go on until late. Mickey also put out a cooler with a few sandwiches and bottled water. If the inspector couldn't come to the party, at the least he could have a snack!

Then Mickey hid several flashlights in different corners of the house. He wanted to be ready in case the lights went out again. In fact, Mickey was pretty sure they would, just as they had in the two parties before. Mickey frowned, concerned, as he remembered what else had happened at the other two parties—precious jewels had been stolen and Minnie ended up in the kitchen, near the back door, in a dead faint. Mickey hoped that neither of those things would happen tonight. The detective was sure that these facts were connected, but he wasn't yet sure how. He refused to believe that Minnie was responsible for the thefts. Then again, all of the other guests were always together in the main room and didn't move once the lights were out. He was sure of that, because in both cases he was the only one who had had the courage to react.

There was only one thing that Mickey was certain of—thinking about this case was giving him a *major* headache.

At around nine, Mickey heard the doorbell. It was Minnie and her guests, Mr. and Mrs. Ruby. Agatha was wearing a magnificent pink organza dress and a splendid diamond choker. She had dyed a few tendrils of her hair to match her dress. Next to Agatha, Minnie looked tired and dreary in a somber blue outfit.

"Minnie!" Mickey called out in greeting. "Do you want to come give me a hand in the kitchen while our guests pour themselves a drink?"

"What?" Minnie asked slowly. Her voice sounded strange and groggy.

"Come to the kitchen with me," Mickey repeated. "I need your help."

"Okay," she said quietly, letting Mickey take her by the hand.

A few minutes later, Mickey and Minnie began receiving guests in the entryway. Everyone had come in their finest clothes. The men were in evening wear with ties and handkerchiefs in their pockets, the women were wrapped in silk and organza (although no one looked half as dressy as Agatha). Each and every one of them wore at least one piece of exquisite jewelry: necklaces, pins, and bracelets. Everyone wanted to prove that

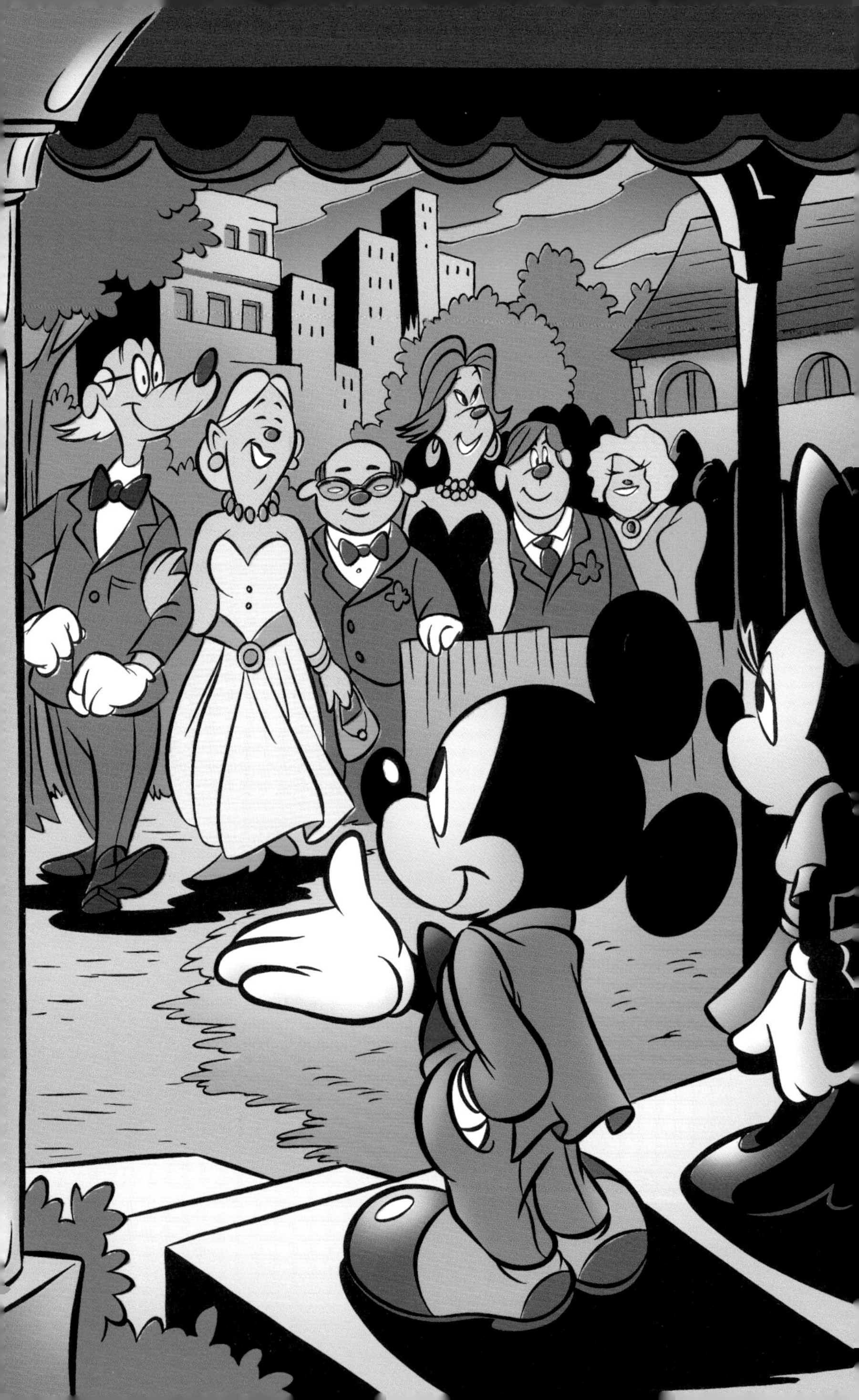

they weren't afraid of a jewel thief—not at Mickey's house.

Determined to throw a great party, Mickey had chosen great dance music and a few of the couples began to dance. Emilio even managed to convince a very pale Minnie to dance a tango. She let herself be led without resisting, moving like a puppet.

Suddenly, at eleven o'clock, the lights went out. The guests were plunged into total darkness and began to murmur anxiously amongst themselves.

In the darkness, Detective Mickey threw himself blindly across the room, reaching for one of the flashlights he had hidden on the bookshelf. It was time to shed a little light on the situation!

Chapter 9

CAUGHT RED-HANDED!

Guided by the swath of light projected by the flashlight, Mickey moved toward the kitchen. He shivered as a current of cold air passed over him: the back door was wide open! Who had passed through there? Had the person come in or gone out? After turning out the flashlight, the detective slowly tiptoed to the door, his heart pounding. He saw the outline of a small figure moving across the lawn. He looked closer. It was Minnie! Suddenly, she stumbled and fell to the ground. Mickey darted through the door.

Once he caught up with his friend, Mickey shook her in an attempt to wake her from her trance. Minnie didn't respond—she had fainted again. Mickey picked up the heavy purse that Minnie had let fall in the grass and slung it over his shoulder. Then he carefully cradled Minnie in his arms and carried her into the kitchen. Behind him, Mickey heard scuffling sounds coming from the garden. . . . But he didn't have time to worry about that now. He had to help Minnie!

As he gently placed her in a chair in the kitchen, Minnie's purse fell to the floor and its contents fell out. Mickey didn't even glance at it.

He peered anxiously at Minnie. She seemed to be in a deep state of sleep. He felt her pulse. It was normal. Her forehead was cool and her breathing was regular. He tickled her elbow lightly, then a little more heavily. Nothing. He tried again. Minnie opened one eye and stared at him.

"It's me, Mickey," he said softly.

"I know," his friend murmured. "What are

we doing here? Why aren't we in the living room with the other guests?"

"Everything's fine, Minnie," Mickey whispered. "Listen, I think somebody's been using you to help them steal jewels—"

Minnie sat bolt upright in her chair. "Mickey, you're out of your mind!" she insisted. "What are you talking about?"

Minnie suddenly became dizzy and she had to put her head between her knees. At that moment that she looked down and saw her purse on the floor. Spilling out of it was a thick roll of money, a gold lighter, and, hidden under everything else, a gorgeous sapphire necklace.

Minnie grew pale. "What—what is this?" she asked in a whisper. "Are you trying to make me think that I was the one who robbed our friends? Is this some kind of bad practical joke?"

Mickey didn't know what to say to that, so he didn't say anything. Clearly, getting Minnie's side of the story was going to be harder than he'd realized. It could wait. Besides, he still had the guests to worry

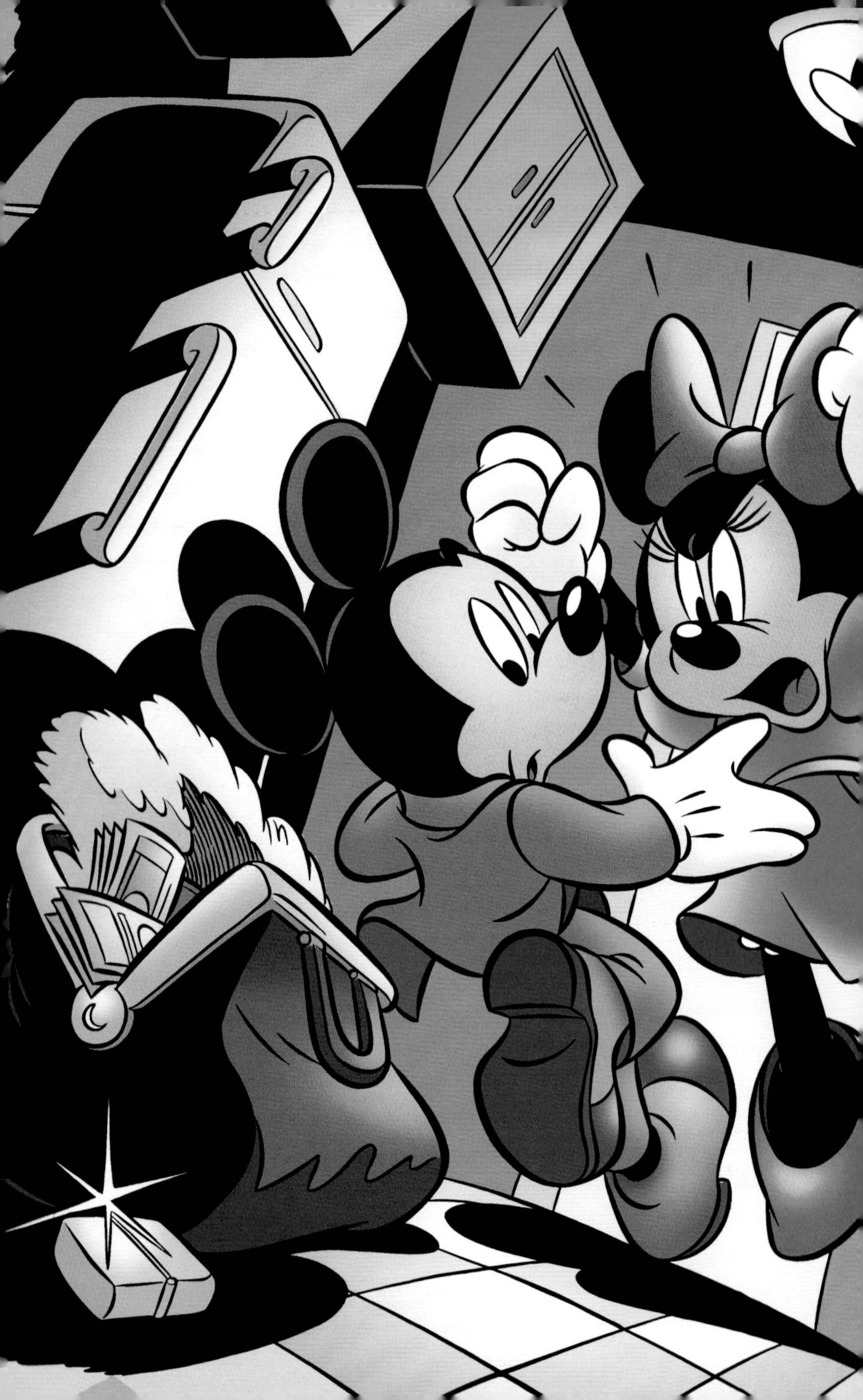

about. They were still in the dark, and he had to figure out what was going on in the garden.

"I wonder what happened to Inspector Swift?" Mickey asked himself as he rushed to the fuse box and turned the electricity back on. He returned to the living room.

"My necklace!" shrieked one of the ladies invited to the party. "It's disappeared!"

Mrs. Rosamond gasped. "That's impossible!" she exclaimed.

"Commissioner! Commissioner!" Mickey interrupted. "Come with me! I heard strange noises—we need to go and see what happened!"

Detective Mickey rushed outside, Commissioner Muttonchops hot on his heels. Once they reached the garden, they found Inspector Swift lying dazed in the grass, tangled up in one of the lawn chairs that Mickey had put outside for his guests.

The commissioner freed him quickly and tried to revive him. But when the officer came to his senses he couldn't remember anything about what had happened.

"Let's go back inside, Commissioner," the detective said. "I don't know who attacked Swift, but I can tell you who committed the robberies!"

Chapter 10

THE MYSTERY UNVEILED

Mickey and Muttonchops, followed by the poor inspector, went back into the living room. The guests observed their entrance in shock. What had happened outside?

Mickey cleared his throat. "My dear friends," he began. "Finally, I've managed to shed some light on the bizarre series of thefts that have occurred in the last few weeks. I needed a little time to figure it out, but now I can tell you for certain who is responsible."

Stupefied whispers rose up from the group of guests. The investigator continued,

"Up until now, we did not have a valid explanation for this series of thefts. Or rather, we had evidence, but the evidence didn't make sense. To all appearances, my good friend Minnie was the guilty one. She was the only link to all three thefts, and I had noticed that her behavior had become suddenly erratic."

"No," Mrs. Rosamond interrupted, "I refuse to believe that Minnie could be responsible!"

Mickey smiled at Minnie's loyal friend. "Yes," he agreed, "I refused to believe it, too. No—Minnie's not the guilty one. I was looking at mug shots of criminals sought by the police when I saw a face, disguised but recognizable, the face of . . . Emilio Ruby!"

Upon hearing Mr. Ruby's name, the guests instinctively shrunk back from the accused magician and his wife. Mr. Ruby turned red as a beet, then stood up from his chair and shook his fist at Mickey. "Who do you think you are?" he demanded. "This is not a party game. I'll teach you to unfairly accuse the innocent without having any proof. Come on, Agatha, let's get out of here. What a humiliation! This is incred—"

"Not so fast!" Mickey interrupted him. "You should know that a detective never makes an accusation without proof. You want proof? Well, here it is. . . ."

Mickey pulled a bunch of postcards from his jacket.

"Explain yourself, Mickey," Muttonchops interrupted. "What do these cards have to do with this case?"

"Here's your explanation, Commissioner. These are the postcards that Minnie has received from Agatha for the last two years." Mickey turned to face his partner, who had appeared in the doorway to the kitchen. "I'm very sorry to have gone through your personal things, Minnie, but I had to keep this part of the investigation secret," Mickey said in a soft voice. "I did it to clear your name." Then he turned back to the guests. "I reconstructed the itinerary of Mr. and Mrs. Ruby, and the time they spent in each city corresponds to the dates of the jewel thefts I looked up on the Internet site for international detectives. Besides, the individuals sought in connection with these thefts all have in common an obsessive love for precious stones, as well as a talent for magic and hypnosis."

Minnie jumped as Mickey pronounced the last word. "Hypnosis!" she cried. "So that's it! When I fainted, I was under Emilio's control. It was Emilio who made me a thief!"

"Please, Minnie, calm down," Mickey told him. "You're not guilty in the least. It's their love of luxury that pushed Agatha and Emilio to turn to crime. They've gotten rich off all the thefts they've committed! It's not by chance that their suitcases feel like they are full of rocks, because in fact they're filled with precious stones. Right, Mrs. Ruby?" Mickey asked as he turned toward Agatha, who was furiously rubbing the hem of her expensive organza dress between her nervous fingers. She responded with an almost imperceptible nod.

"So," Mickey went on, "I've also been trying to figure out who had knocked Goofy to the ground in front of Minnie's house. I realized once I saw the police photographs that it was none other than Emilio, who had come to do his first test on Minnie to make sure the hypnosis would work. Of course, the reason Goofy and I didn't see Emilio and Agatha on the platform that day when we went to pick them up at the train station. They never got off the train! They had already been in the city, and simply walked to the nearest platform to be picked up. As in the other cities where they've operated, Emilio had decided to hypnotize an innocent person to make her commit the crimes so that he would not be accused himself. Then, once the thefts were complete, they would leave the city and assume new identities. That way, they stayed one step ahead of the police. . . . Until now."

"And how did Emilio manage to hypnotize his victims?" Muttonchops asked.

"There's really nothing magic about his method at all. I did some research, and found out that it takes only one session to render someone completely obedient. Then it's enough to repeat a short phrase in a low voice to reactivate the hypnotic effect. The victim will then do whatever she's told without a second thought."

"So Mr. Ruby hypnotized Minnie and used her to carry out the thefts during the parties," Muttonchops concluded.

"Exactly," Mickey responded. "Minnie's symptoms—fatigue and nervousness—correspond perfectly to the effects of long-term hypnosis."

Commissioner Muttonchops frowned and turned to Emilio. "In the name of the law," he announced in a harsh voice, "Emilio Ruby, or whoever you are, you are under arrest. Agents, the handcuffs, please. This time he won't manage to weasel his way out."

"You can't do this to me!" Emilio cried. "Your arguments don't make any sense! Why would I steal the jewels from my own wife? Or did Minnie manage to get into the magic box herself?"

"No—I suspect that Minnie just turned off the electricity in that incident. Then, Agatha hid her jewels herself," Mickey retorted.

"Come on, Mickey. Give us the full explanation," Muttonchops exclaimed.

"From the moment I understood that you were the guilty one," Mickey continued as he

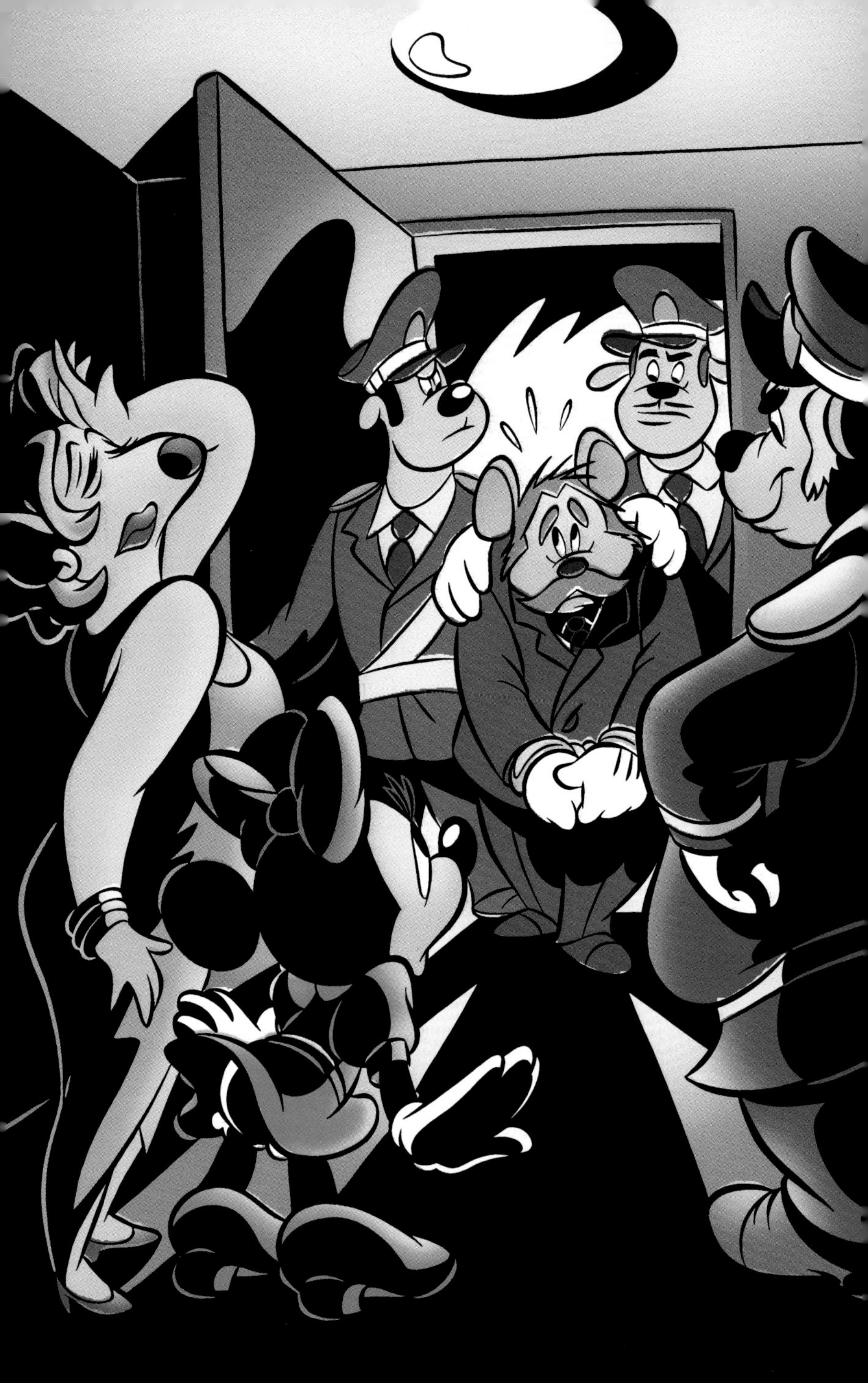

turned to Emilio, "I tried to discover where you had hidden your little treasure trove. I began a careful exploration of the places where the thefts took place, but with no success. I thought that perhaps you were hiding the valuable objects in Minnie's room. But I checked myself and found nothing. So I realized that you must be getting rid of the jewels halfway between where the crime was committed and Minnie's house."

"Excuse me, Mickey . . . between the houses where the thefts took place and Minnie's house there is nothing but a bunch of flower beds and a bus stop," Goofy put in.

"Exactly. But looking with a bit more attention, you can see also a recycling container for cans near the garbage can at the bus stop, an ideal place for hiding something you don't want anyone to find. No one wants to go around sticking their nose where the trash can is! All those two rascals had to do was slip the jewels in and then wait until it was time to leave to go and retrieve them and escape!"

"But the city garbage collectors might've

carried them away!" the commissioner cried. "Perhaps it's even too late for us to retrieve them!"

"Don't worry, Commissioner!" Mickey reassured him. "Emilio had calculated everything perfectly. The garbage collectors retrieve cans only once every two weeks, on Saturday morning, to be exact. And all the thefts occurred between the Sunday before last and this evening. Today is Friday and tomorrow is collection day. Emilio was planning to retrieve his treasures right before leaving the city tonight, without risking that they would end up in a garbage incinerator."

"But, Mickey," Minnie protested, tears in her eyes, "*I* was the only one caught red-handed. These thieves have ruined me!"

Mickey put a comforting arm around his friend. "Don't worry, Minnie," he said. "You were just a victim. Emilio is the one who will be held responsible for the crimes. When he saw that you responded so well to his hypnotic techniques, he wanted to exploit you as much as he could. He wanted you to be the one to put the purse with the money and jewels into the recycling container. This time, however, he went too far. Simple, isn't it?"

Commissioner Muttonchops couldn't hide his admiration for Mickey's detective work. "Congratulations, Mickey!" he said heartily. "You really outdid yourself this time. What great instincts!"

"I did it all to protect Minnie's good reputation. Emilio would never have been able to hypnotize her if she hadn't had complete faith in Agatha."

Mrs. Ruby stood up and with a theatrical gesture advanced toward the police officer.

"Commissioner," she exclaimed, "I confess my guilt. Put the handcuffs on me. Yes, it's true, Emilio is a criminal. And since I didn't have the courage to turn him in, I have become his accomplice. And besides, I just love jewelry, and I can't resist a beautiful evening gown. But please know, my friends, that I do not take what I have done lightly. . . ."

Minnie collapsed into an armchair, suddenly overwhelmed by exhaustion. How could her teacher—her role model—have used her this way? And what did her good friends think of her, now that she'd been involved in these crimes? Minnie felt like crying.

Mickey ran to her side to console her. "Don't worry, it's all over," he said gently. "It's tomorrow, Minnie! It's Saturday!"

"So?" his friend sighed.

"Soooo . . ." Mickey said, waggling his eyebrows, "it's your birthday! Or did you forget?"

Minnie laughed through her tears. "I can't believe it," she said. "I've been so busy with Agatha and her husband that I even forgot my own birthday!"

EPILOGUE

The next day, at lunchtime, Mickey and Goofy met in front of Minnie's house. At the first ring of the doorbell they heard her footsteps. When she opened the door she was all smiles. Mickey offered her two tickets: the reservations for their trip to Enigma. The birthday girl read the brochure eagerly.

"It's amazing! A trip to the famous mystery park . . . what a surprise!" Minnie said eagerly. "So am I back to being a trusty partner to my favorite detective?"

"I never doubted you, Minnie," Mickey said sincerely.

Minnie smiled. "Thank you, Mickey," she said, "for everything." She looked down shyly, then said, "Well, I guess it's time for lunch. I'm starved!" Minnie hurried to the kitchen, then returned with a plate of sandwiches, which the friends helped themselves to eagerly.

"There's still one thing that I don't quite understand," Minnie said as her friends munched away happily. "Last night, Emilio and I didn't know that Inspector Swift was in the garden. And then he was found later, sprawled out in a lawn chair. So what happened to him?"

Mickey nodded. "It's the only unanswered question," he agreed. "I think we're going to have a tough time explaining it. His version of events is so confusing. . . ."

Goofy, who had remained silent until that moment, timidly interrupted, "Er—I have a confession to make. . . ."

Mickey looked interested. "Do you know something about this, Goofy?" he asked.

"To tell you the truth . . . um . . ." Goofy said awkwardly, "I did it."

"What?" Minnie's eyes were wide.

"Aw garsh," Goofy said, blushing. "I was in the yard when the lights went out. I saw someone's shadow near the hedge, and thought it was the thief. So I snuck up behind him and tripped him—I didn't realize it was the inspector!"

"Well, Goofy," Mickey said slowly. "I appreciate that you were trying to help. But . . . poor Inspector Swift!"

"Yes, well, I'm sorry about that. And I'll apologize to Inspector Swift, too," he added, "as soon as I figure out how! Well, Minnie, thanks for a delicious lunch." Goofy pushed his chair back and stood up. "I'm sorry, but I have to go. I'm expecting some out-of-town visitors!"

"Really?" Minnie asked him with a smile. "Who?"

"Oh, it's a long story!" Goofy replied. "They were both my teachers in elementary school and we kept in touch."

Minnie and Mickey gaped at him a moment. Then they started to laugh. After all, how many teachers could turn into jewel thieves and come to town in one month?

Right?